MEMOIRS OF A WOMAN DOCTOR

MEMOIRS OF A WOMAN DOCTOR

A novel by Nawal El Saadawi

Translated from the Arabic by Catherine Cobham

CITY LIGHTS BOOKS
San Francisco

First City Lights Books edition 1989
Copyright © 1988 by Saqi Books
First published 1988 by Saqi Books, U.K.

Cover illustration by Axelle Fortier
Cover design by Patricia Fujii

Library of Congress Cataloging-in-Publication Data

Sa dawi, Nawal.
  [Mudhakkirāt tabībah. English]
  Memoirs of a woman doctor : a novel / by Nawal el Saadawi :
  translated by Catherine Cobham.
    p. cm.
  Translation of : Mudhakkirat tabıbah.
  ISBN: 0-87286-223-2 / ISBN 13: 978-0-87286-223-4
  I. Title
PJ7862.A3M813   1989
892'.736--dc19
                                        89-957
                                        CIP

Visit our website: www.citylights.com

CITY LIGHTS BOOKS are edited by Lawrence Ferlinghetti and
Nancy J. Peters and published at the City Lights Bookstore,
261 Columbus Avenue, San Francisco, CA 94133.

Author's Note

I wrote *Memoirs of a Woman Doctor* thirty years ago when, as a young woman in my twenties, I had just graduated from the School of Medicine in Cairo. It expressed my feelings and experiences as a woman who was a doctor at work, but still performed the roles of a wife and a mother at home.

Memoirs first appeared in serialized form in the Egyptian magazine *Ruz al-Yusuf* in 1957. It had a great impact in Egypt and in the Arab world. Some critics regarded it as a revolutionary feminist novel which revealed the double exploitation of Egyptian women — both their general, social oppression and their private oppression through the institution of marriage. But the book was also controversial. *Ruz al-Yusuf* deleted sections of the complete work from the serialized version on the demand of the government censor. I then tried to have the book published without deletions but publishers refused to print it without censoring it. As I was young and inexperienced and eager to see the book in print, I allowed it to be published with deletions.

Since that time, the novel has been frequently reprinted in both Cairo and Beirut. But it has never appeared in its entirety because I have lost the original manuscript.

Despite these limitations, I still consider *Memoirs*, incomplete as it is in the present edition, as a fair description of the moral and social position of women in that period. Some people believe that *Memoirs* is autobiographical, but although many of the heroine's characteristics fit those of an Egyptian woman such as myself, active in the medical field in those years, the work is still fiction. It is one thing to write a novel, and another to write one's autobiography.

At that time I had not read any feminist literature on women's struggles or on women's status in contemporary society — this only came later — but although I have subsequently written many novels and short stories which may be more sophisticated, I still consider *Memoirs* like a first daughter, full of youthful fervour and expressing a reality which is still relevant today. It is a simple, spontaneous novel in which there is a lot of anger against the oppression of women in my country, but also a great deal of hope for change, for wider horizons and a better future.

Nawal el-Saadawi
London, June 1987

8

1

The conflict between me and my femininity began very early on, before my female characteristics had become pronounced and before I knew anything about myself, my sex and my origins, indeed before I knew the nature of the cavity which had housed me before I was expelled into the wide world.

All I did know at that time was that I was a girl. I used to hear it from my mother all day long. 'Girl!' she would call, and all it meant to me was that I wasn't a boy and I wasn't like my brother.

My brother's hair was cut short but otherwise left free and uncombed, while mine was allowed to grow longer and longer and my mother combed it twice a day and twisted it into plaits and imprisoned the ends of it in ribbons and rubber bands.

My brother woke up in the morning and left his bed just as it was, while I had to make my bed and his as well.

My brother went out into the street to play without asking my parents' permission and came back whenever he liked, while I could only go out if and when they let me.

My brother took a bigger piece of meat than me, gobbled it up and drank his soup noisily and my mother never said a word. But I was different: I was a girl. I had to watch every movement I made, hide my longing for the food, eat slowly and drink my soup without a sound.

My brother played, jumped around and turned somersaults, whereas if I ever sat down and allowed my skirt to ride as much as a centimetre up my thighs, my mother would pierce me with a glance like an animal immobilizing its prey and I would cover up those shameful parts of my body.

Shameful! Everything in me was shameful and I was a child of just nine years old.

I felt sorry for myself and locked myself in my room and cried. The first real tears I shed in my life weren't because I'd done badly at school or broken something valuable but because I was a girl. I wept over my femininity even before I knew what it was. The moment I opened my eyes on life, a state of enmity already existed between me and my nature.

★ ★ ★ ★

I jumped down the stairs three at a time so as to be in the street before I'd counted ten. My brother and some of the boys and girls who lived nearby were waiting for me to play cops and robbers. I'd asked my mother's permission. I loved playing games and running as fast as I could. I felt an overwhelming happiness as I moved my head and arms and legs in the air or broke into a series of leaps and bounds, constrained only by the weight of my body which was dragged down earthwards time and again.

Why had God created me a girl and not a bird flying in the air like that pigeon? It seemed to me that God must prefer birds to girls. But my brother couldn't fly and this consoled me a little. I realized that despite his great freedom he was as incapable as I was of flying. I began to search constantly for weak spots in males to console me for the powerlessness imposed on me by the fact of being female.

I was bounding ecstatically along when I felt a violent shudder running through my body. My head spun and I saw something red. I didn't know what had happened to me. Fear gripped my heart and I left the game. I ran back to the house and locked myself in the bathroom to investigate the secret of this grave event in private.

I didn't understand it at all. I thought I must have been struck down by a terrible illness. I went to ask my mother about it in fear and trembling and saw laughter and happiness written all over her face. I wondered in amazement how she could greet this affliction with such a broad smile. Noticing my surprise and confusion, she took me by the hand and led me to my room. Here she told me women's bloody tale.

I took to my room for four days running. I couldn't face my brother, my father or even the house-boy. I thought they must all have been told about the shameful thing that had happened to me: my mother would doubtless have revealed my new secret. I locked myself in, trying to come to terms with this phenomenon. Was this unclean procedure the only way for girls to reach maturity? Could a human being really live for several days at the mercy of involuntary muscular activity? God must really hate girls to have tarnished them with this curse. I felt that God had favoured boys in everything.

I got up from the bed, dragged myself over to the mirror and looked at the two little mounds sprouting on my chest. If only I could die! I didn't recognize this body which sprang a new shame on me every day, adding to my weakness and my preoccupation with myself. What would grow on my body next? What other new symptom would my tyrannical femininity break out in?

★ ★ ★ ★

I hated being female. I felt as if I was in chains — chains forged from my own blood tying me to the bed so that I couldn't run and jump, chains produced by the cells of my own body, chains of shame and humiliation. I turned in on myself to cover up my miserable existence.

I no longer went out to run and play. The two mounds on my chest were growing bigger. They bounced gently as I walked. I was unhappy with my tall slender frame, folding my arms over my chest to

12

hide it and looking sadly at my brother and his friends as they played.

I grew. I grew taller than my brother even though he was older than me. I grew taller than the other children of my age. I withdrew from their midst and sat alone thinking. My childhood was over, a brief, breathless childhood. I'd scarcely been aware of it before it was gone, leaving me with a mature woman's body carrying deep inside it a ten-year-old child.

★ ★ ★ ★

I saw the doorman's eyes and teeth shining in his black face as he came up to me; I was sitting alone on his wooden bench letting my eyes follow the movements of my brother and his friends in the street. I felt the rough edge of his galabiya brushing my leg and breathed in the strange smell of his clothes. I edged away in disgust. As he came closer again, I tried to hide my fear by staring fixedly at my brother and his companions as they played, but I felt his coarse rough fingers stroking my leg and moving up under my clothes. I jumped up in alarm and raced away from him. This horrible man had noticed my womanhood as well! I ran all the way up to our flat and my mother asked what the matter was. But I couldn't tell her anything, perhaps out of a feeling of fear or humiliation or a mixture of the two. Or perhaps because I thought she'd scold me and that would put an end to the special affection between us that made me tell her my secrets.

★ ★ ★ ★

I no longer went out in the street, and I didn't sit on the wooden bench any more. I fled from those strange creatures with harsh voices and moustaches, the creatures they called men. I created an imaginary private world for myself in which I was a goddess and men were stupid, helpless creatures at my beck and call. I sat on a high throne in this world of mine, arranging the dolls on chairs, making the boys sit on the floor and telling stories to myself. Alone with my imagination and my dolls, nobody ruffled the calm of my life, except my mother with her never-ending orders for me to do tasks around the flat or in the kitchen: the hateful, constricted world of women with its permanent reek of garlic and onions. I'd scarcely retreated into my own little world when my mother would drag me into the kitchen saying, 'You're going to be married one day. You must learn how to cook. You're going to be married…' Marriage! Marriage! That loathsome word which my mother mentioned every day until I hated the sound of it. I couldn't hear it without having a mental picture of a man with a big see-through belly with a table of food inside it. In my mind the smell of the kitchen was linked with the smell of a husband and I hated the word husband just as I hated the smell of the food we cooked.

★ ★ ★ ★

14

My grandmother's chatter broke off as she looked at my chest. I saw her diseased old eyes scrutinizing the two sprouting buds and evaluating them. Then she whispered something to my mother and I heard my mother saying to me, 'Put on your cream dress and go and say hello to your father's guest in the sitting-room.'

I caught a whiff of conspiracy in the air. I was used to meeting most of my father's friends and bringing them coffee. Sometimes I sat with them and heard my father telling them how well I was doing at school. This always made me feel elated and I thought that since my father had acknowledged my intelligence he would extricate me from the depressing world of women, reeking of onions and marriage.

But why the cream dress? It was new and I hated it. It had a strange gather at the front which made my breasts look larger. My mother looked at me inquiringly and asked, 'Where's your cream dress?'

'I won't wear it,' I replied angrily.

She noticed the stirrings of rebellion in my eyes and said regretfully, 'Smooth down your eyebrows then.'

I didn't look at her, and before opening the sitting-room door I ruffled up my eyebrows with my fingers.

I greeted my father's friend and sat down. I saw a strange, frightening face and eyes examining me relentlessly as my grandmother's had done shortly before.

'She's first in her group at primary school this year,' said my father.

I didn't notice any admiration in the man's eyes at these words but I saw his inquiring glances roaming all over my body before coming to rest on my chest. Scared, I stood up and ran out of the room as if a devil was after me. My mother and grandmother met me eagerly at the door and asked in unison, 'What did you do?'

I let out a single cry in their faces and ran to my room, slamming the door behind me. Then I went over to the mirror and stared at my chest. I hated them, these two protrusions, these two lumps of flesh which were determining my future! How I wished I could cut them off with a sharp knife! But I couldn't. All I could do was hide them by flattening them with a tight corset.

★ ★ ★ ★

The heavy long hair I carried around everywhere on my head held me up in the morning, got in my way in the bath and made my neck burning hot in the summer. Why wasn't it short and free like my brother's? His didn't weigh his head down or hinder his activities. But it was my mother who controlled my life, my future and my body right down to every strand of my hair. Why? Because she'd given birth to me? But why did that give her some special merit? She went about her normal life like any other woman and conceived me involuntarily in a random moment of pleasure. I'd arrived without her knowing or choosing me, and without my choosing her. We'd been thrust arbitrarily on one another as mother and daughter. Could any human being love someone who'd been forced upon them? And if my mother loved me instinctively in spite of herself, what credit did that do her? Did it make her any better than a cat which sometimes loves its kittens and at other times devours them? I sometimes thought the harsh way she treated me hurt me more than if she'd eaten me! If she really loved me and wanted my happiness above her own, then why did her demands and desires always work against my happiness? How could she possibly love me when she put chains on my arms and legs and round my neck every day?

★ ★ ★ ★

For the first time in my life I left the flat without asking my mother's permission. My heart was pounding as I went down the street, though my provocative act had given me a certain strength. As I walked, a sign caught my eye: 'Ladies' Hairdresser'. I had only a second's hesitation before going in.

I watched the long tresses squirm in the jaws of the sharp scissors and then fall to the ground. Were these what my mother called a woman's crowning glory? Could a woman's crown fall shattered to the ground like this because of one moment of determination? I was filled with a great contempt for womankind: I had seen with my own eyes that women believe in worthless trivia. This contempt gave me added strength. I walked back home with a firm step and stood squarely in front of my mother with my newly cropped hair.

My mother gave a shrill cry and slapped my face hard. Then she hit me again and again while I stood where I was as if rooted to the spot. My challenging of authority had turned me into an immovable force, my victory over my mother had transformed me into a solid mass, unaffected by the assault. My mother's hand struck my face and then drew back each time, as if it had hit a granite boulder.

Why didn't I cry? I usually burst into tears at the slightest snub or the gentlest of slaps. But the tears didn't come. My eyes stayed open, looking into my mother's eyes boldly and firmly. She went on slapping me for a while, then collapsed back on to the sofa, repeating in bewilderment, 'You must have gone mad!'

I felt sorry for her when I saw her features crumbling in helpless defeat. I had a strong urge to hug and kiss her and break down and cry in her arms, and say to her, 'It's not good for me always to do as you say.'

But I took my eyes away from hers so she wouldn't realize I'd witnessed her defeat, and ran off to my room. I looked in the mirror and smiled at my short hair, the light of victory in my eyes.

For the first time in my life I understood the meaning of victory; fear led only to defeat, and victory demanded courage. My fear of my mother had vanished; that great aura which had made me terrified of her had fallen away. I realized that she was just an ordinary woman. The slaps she delivered were the strongest thing about her but they no longer scared me — because they didn't hurt any more.

★ ★ ★ ★

I hated our flat except for the room where my books were. I loved school except for the home economics period. I loved all the days of the week except Friday.

I took part in all school activities and joined the drama society, the debating society, the athletics club, and the music and art clubs. Even that wasn't enough for me so I got together with some friends and we set up a society that I called the Friendship Club. Why, I'm not sure, except that deep down inside I had an overwhelming longing for companionship, for profound, all-embracing companionship with no strings attached, for vast groups of people to be with me, talk to me, listen to me and soar up to the heavens with me.

It seemed to me that whatever heights I reached, I wouldn't be content, the flame burning within me wouldn't be extinguished. I began to hate the repetitiveness and similarity of lessons: I would read the material once and once only — to go over it again would stifle me, kill me. I wanted something new, new... all the time.

★ ★ ★ ★

I wasn't aware of him at first when he came into my room where I sat reading and stood beside me. Then he said, 'Don't you want to relax for a bit?'

I'd been reading for ages and felt tired so I smiled and said, 'I'd like to go for a walk in the fresh air.'

'Put on your coat and let's go.'

I quickly pulled on my coat and ran to catch up with him. I was on the point of slipping my hand into his and running along together as we used to do when we were children. But then I caught his eye and suddenly remembered how many years it had been since I had last played like a child, years during which my legs had forgotten how to run and become used to moving slowly like grown-ups' legs. I put my hand in my coat pocket and walked slowly at his side.

'You've grown,' he said.

'So have you.'

'Do you remember when we used to play together?'

'You always beat me when we had races.'

'You always won at marbles.'

We laughed uproariously. The air flooded into my chest and invigorated me, making me feel as if I was recapturing something denied to me in my over-regimented childhood.

'I bet I'd win if we had a race now.'

'No, I'll beat you,' I said confidently.

'Let's see.'

We marked out a line on the ground and stood side by side. He shouted, 'One... two... three...' and we shot forward. I was about to reach the goal first when he grabbed my clothes from behind. I stumbled and fell and he fell beside me. Still panting, I looked up at him and saw him staring at me in a funny way which made the blood rush to my cheeks. I watched his arm reach out in the direction of my waist and he whispered in a rough voice, 'I'm going to kiss you.'

I was convulsed by a strange and violent trembling. For a moment which passed like lightning through my feelings, I wished he would stretch out his arm further and hold me tight, but then this odd secret desire was transformed into a wild fury.

My anger only made him more persistent and he held on to me with an iron grip. I don't know where I got the strength, but I threw off his arm and it flailed in the air while I brought my hand down hard across his face.

★ ★ ★ ★

I turned over and over in bed in utter confusion. Strange sensations swept through me and images flashed before my eyes. One of them lodged itself in front of me and wouldn't go away: my cousin lying on the ground beside me, his arm nearly round my waist and his strange glances boring into my head. I closed my eyes and was borne along by my fantasy in which his arms moved tightly round me and his lips pressed firmly down on mine.

I buried my head under the covers, unable to believe that I'd slapped him with the hand I was now picturing quivering in his. I pulled the covers tightly over my head to shut out my strange dream but it crept back, so I put the pillow over my head and pressed it down as hard as I could to suffocate the stubborn ghost, until sleep finally overtook me.

★ ★ ★ ★

I opened my eyes the following morning. The sunlight had chased away the darkness and all the phantoms that prowled in its shadows. I opened the window and the fresh air blew in, chasing away the last clinging traces of the night's dreams. I smiled scornfully at the cowardly part of me which trembled with fear at the stronger part when I was awake, but then crept into my bed at night and filled the darkness around me with fantasies and illusions.

In my final year at secondary school I came out top of my group... I sat wondering what to do...

I hated my femininity, resented my nature and knew nothing about my body. All that was left for me was to reject, to challenge, to resist! I would reject my femininity, challenge my nature, resist all the desires of my body; prove to my mother and grandmother that I wasn't a woman like them, that I wouldn't spend my life in the kitchen peeling onions and garlic, wasting all my days so that my husband could eat and eat.

I was going to show my mother that I was more intelligent than my brother, than the man she'd wanted me to wear the cream dress for, than any man, and that I could do everything my father did and more.

2

The faculty of medicine? Yes, medicine... The word had a terrifying effect on me. It reminded me of penetrating eyes moving at an amazing speed behind shiny steel-rimmed spectacles, and strong pointed fingers holding a dreadful long sharp needle. I remembered the first time I'd ever seen a doctor: my mother was trembling with fright, looking up at him beseechingly and reverently; my brother was terrified; my father was lying in bed begging for help. Medicine was a terrifying thing. It inspired respect, even veneration, in my mother and brother and father. I would become a doctor then, study medicine, wear shiny steel-rimmed spectacles, make my eyes move at an amazing speed behind them, and make my fingers strong and pointed to hold the dreadful long sharp needle. I'd make my mother tremble with fright and look at me reverently; I'd make my brother terrified and my father beg me for help. I'd prove to nature that I could overcome the disadvantages of the frail body she'd clothed me in, with its shameful parts both inside and out. I would imprison it in the steel cell forged from my will and my intelligence. I wouldn't give it a single chance to drag me into the ranks of illiterate women.

★ ★ ★ ★

I stood in the courtyard of the faculty of medicine, looking about me. Hundreds of eyes directed sharp questioning glances at me. I looked squarely back at them. Why should I lower my eyes when they looked at me, bow my head while they were lifting theirs, stumble along while they walked with a proud and confident step? I was the same as them, or better. I drew myself up to my full height. I'd forgotten about my breasts and their weight on my chest had vanished. I felt light, as if I could move as easily and freely as I wanted. I had charted my way in life, the way of the mind. I had carried out the death sentence on my body so that I no longer felt it existed.

★ ★ ★ ★

I stood at the door of the dissecting room: a surprisingly penetrating smell... naked human corpses on white marble slabs. My feet carried me in fearfully. I went up to one of the naked corpses and stood beside it. It was a man's body, completely naked. The students were looking at me, smiling slyly and waiting to see what I would do. I almost turned away and ran out, but no, I wasn't going to do that. On my other side I saw a woman's naked body surrounded by a cluster of students inspecting it boldly and without shame. I turned my gaze back to the man's corpse and examined it steadily and unflinchingly, taking the scalpel in my hand.

★ ★ ★ ★

This was my first encounter with a naked man, and in the course of it men lost their dread power and illusory greatness in my eyes. A man had fallen from his throne and lay on a dissecting table next to a woman. Why had my mother made all these tremendous distinctions between me and my brother, and portrayed man as a god whom I would have to serve in the kitchen all my life? Why had society always tried to convince me that manhood was a distinction and an honour, and womanhood a weakness and a disgrace? Would my mother ever believe that I'd stood with a naked man in front of me and a knife in my hand, and opened up his stomach and his head? Would society believe that I'd examined a man's body and taken it to pieces without caring that it was a man?

Who was this society anyway? Wasn't it men like my brother brought up from childhood to think of themselves as gods, and weak, ineffectual women like my mother? How could such people believe that there existed a woman who knew nothing about a man except that he was an assortment of muscles, arteries, nerves and bones?

A man's body! The terror of mothers and little girls who sweltered in the heat of the kitchen to fill it with food, and carried the spectre of it with them day and night. Here was just such a body spread out before me naked, ugly and in pieces. I hadn't imagined that life would prove my mother wrong so soon, or give me my revenge in this way over that miserable man who'd looked at my breasts one day and not seen anything else of me besides them. Here I was slinging his arrows straight back into his chest. Here I was looking at his naked body and feeling nauseated, tearing him to shreds with my scalpel.

Was this a man's body, the outside covered with hair and the inside full of decaying stinking organs, his brain floating in a sticky white fluid and his heart in thick red blood? How ugly man was, both inside and out... as ugly as could be!

★ ★ ★ ★

I examined the young woman lying under my scalpel on the white marble table. Her long hair was soft and dyed red but it had been washed in formalin. Her teeth were white and shiny, with a gold one at the front, but they were all yellow near the roots; her breasts were drooping and skinny. Those two pieces of flesh which had tormented me in childhood, which determined girls' futures and inflamed men's eyes and minds, had come to rest shrivelled and dried up like a piece of old shoe leather. How lacking in substance were girls' futures, how insignificant that which filled the hearts and eyes of men! And the long shiny hair that my mother had plagued me with — woman's

26

crowning glory which she carries on her head and wastes half her life arranging, shining and dyeing — fell into the filthy bin along with other unwanted bodily matter and scraps of flesh.

★ ★ ★ ★

I felt a sour taste in my throat and spat out the piece of meat from my mouth. I tried to chew on a piece of bread but my teeth moved with difficulty. I tried to swallow and felt the bread scraping against the walls of my larynx and down into my stomach. I felt the acid juices secreted by my stomach walls working on the bread and my intestine expanding to receive it. I felt something weighing down on my chest and knew it was my heart pumping, chasing the blood into the arteries. I felt the blood creeping back along my veins and the faint pulsating of the capillaries in my limbs. I felt the air entering my nostrils and passing down my throat to fill my lungs. They expanded like balloons until the air stopped coming into my chest and I seemed to be choking. My lips stopped moving, I couldn't stretch out my arms, the muscles of my heart weren't contracting and my veins were no longer throbbing with blood.

Ah, I'd died! I jumped up in fright...

No, I wasn't going to die! I refused to join all the corpses stretched out in front of me on the tables. I put down my scalpel and raced out of the dissecting room. In the street I looked around me in astonishment as people walked and moved their arms and legs without a moment's thought, running easily to catch buses, opening their mouths and moving their lips and talking and breathing without the slightest difficulty.

I calmed down. Life went on and I was still alive. I opened my mouth wide and filled my lungs with the air of the street and breathed in deeply. I moved my arms and legs and walked in the midst of the surging mass of humanity. Ah, how simple life is when one takes it as it comes!

★ ★ ★ ★

A small roundish object, an egg-shaped piece of flesh, was quivering under my scalpel. I took hold of it in one hand and put it on the scales. I felt it with the tips of my fingers; its surface was soft and convoluted, just like the rabbit's brain which I'd dug out of its little skull on the table earlier. Was it possible that this was the brain of a human being? Could this piece of moist tender flesh be the mighty human mind that had triumphed over nature and gone down into the bowels of the earth and up into orbit with the sun and moon, which could split rocks and move mountains and extract enough fire from atoms to destroy the world?

I seized the scalpel and cut the brain up into pieces, then the pieces into still more pieces. I looked and felt and probed and found nothing. Only a piece of soft flesh which disintegrated under my fingers.

I put a sliver of it under the microscope and saw

nothing but round cells containing round nuclei like bunches of grapes. How did they work and make people aware and able to understand and feel? I opened the textbook and looked at the illustrations showing the workings of the brain. They were like drawings of complicated machinery, a television, an aircraft or a submarine, or like a map of the world: hundreds of transmitting and receiving posts, millions of nerves and thread-like filaments and I knew that the piece of flesh in my hand was in charge of all this. It received messages from all the organs of the body and then sent orders to them through strings of nerves. How could this be, this little ball of flesh giving orders to the heart, the arms, the legs; saying to the heart 'Move', to the arms 'Go down' or 'Come up', to the legs 'Walk' or 'Stop'? How could this whole interwoven network of nerve cells operate without crashing into each other? What made it decode the secret of the messages sent to it by the eye, the nose, the ear, the tongue, the fingertips, without confusing them with each other? I looked back at the little round cells through the microscope and wondered again how life could invade these minute amounts of protoplasm and move and understand and know.

I opened my textbooks to look into this mystery. The chemistry books said that there may be chemical reactions which modify and activate the components of the substance. The physics books talked of electricity altering its atoms and releasing life, and the physiology book spoke of reflexes and secretions.

I began to read and search and probe until I'd learnt the structure and organization of the human body by heart. I learnt the names of all the parts of the nervous system and the way the nerve cells transmit messages around the body; the names of the veins and arteries, how long and broad they were, what sort of walls they had; the make-up of bones, bone marrow and blood; how I ate; how all my senses functioned; and how I slept and dreamt. I discovered how my heart beat and why I blushed; how I felt fire burning and how to draw my hand away from it; why I sweated with embarrassment and why my extremities turned cold through fear.

The heart was like a house: it had rooms with muscle-walls and valve-doors; the walls of one room contracted and its doors opened and forced the blood out of it into the next room whose muscular walls were relaxed, then the valve-door closed... The heartbeats were the small noises made by the blood going from one room to another and the doors opening and shutting. But how did the heart muscles know when to contract and when to relax? A message! A telegram transmitted to them by a nerve connected to a centre in the chest, which led in turn to one of the centres in the brain. How did the blood from the lungs reach the heart and how did it go back once more to the lungs to be purified? It was all controlled by a precise and strict system. Every cavity in the body had a special membrane and the blood pressure was strictly regulated as it passed ceaselessly from vessel to vessel.

Why did I feel fire burning my finger? Because the nerve endings in my fingers transmitted a message to the brain, which interpreted it as being a pain caused by burning and sent a rapid message to my arm muscles ordering them to contract and take my finger away from the fire. Who would have thought that these messages could flow back and forth between the fingertips and the brain in the time it takes us to remove our fingers from the heat which is burning them?

I didn't sweat from embarrassment until negotiations had taken place between the nerve centres in my brain and my sweat glands, culminating in the brain ordering the glands to shed their drops of moisture.

My extremities didn't get cold until the fear had been signalled to my brain and it had given the order to the blood vessels at the surface of my skin to shrink so that the blood left them ready to deal with any possible injury.

I learnt how images and sounds were transmitted to the brain from the eye and the ear. And how living organisms became bread, an inanimate substance, in the heat of the oven, and how this was then converted to living tissue in the warmth of human insides.

I learnt that while I slept, part of my brain remained alert and conscious, watching over my heartbeats and whispered breathing and controlling my dream pictures. It saved me from falling out of bed when I flew on the back of a charger up into the sky, or fell through the air and drowned in the roaring ocean. And it woke me up before I wet the bed in fright when a demon of the forest sunk his teeth into my flesh.

A vast new world opened up before me. At first I was apprehensive, but I soon plunged avidly into it, overwhelmed by a frenzied passion for knowledge. Science revealed the secrets of human existence to me and made nonsense of the huge differences which my mother had tried to construct between me and my brother.

Science proved to me that women were like men and men like animals. A woman had a heart, a nervous system and a brain exactly like a man's, and an animal had a heart, a nervous system and a brain exactly like a human being's. There were no essential differences between them! A woman contained a man inside her and a man concealed a woman in his depths. A woman had male organs, some apparent and some hidden, and a man had female hormones in his blood. Human beings had truncated tails in the form of a few little vertebrae at the base of their spinal columns; and animals shed tears.

I was delighted by this new world which placed men, women and the animals side by side, and by science which seemed a mighty, just and omniscient god; so I placed my trust in it and embraced its teachings.

★ ★ ★ ★

All I could see of him was his little face, his eyes searching desperately for some sign of sympathy and his thin bare arms trembling with cold. His body was completely hidden under hard metal discs with rubber tubes protruding from them, ending in human ears that looked like rabbits' ears. The stethoscopes were raised momentarily to reveal parts of his bare chest but others quickly came down in their place; some were held in rough, swollen fingers, others in soft hands with red-painted finger nails, and they compressed his childish ribs with the cold metal.

I heard the professor's voice saying, 'Come and listen to these heartbeats.'

The hands of my fellow students crowding round the sick child pushed me forward and I stood waiting with the stethoscope attached to my ears until a small space became vacant on the thin body. I saw the round red indentation left by the previous instrument; my own swayed uncertainly in my hand and I found it impossible to place it on the inflamed body; my hand began to shake uncontrollably. At that moment I was pushed roughly aside and the crowd of students swept me back from the bed. A student wearing thick glasses took my place and jammed his stethoscope unhesitatingly on to the child's chest as if he hadn't seen the angry circle there. A feeble complaint broke from the child's dry lips and went unheard in the noisy crowd competing for a place around his sickbed.

I suppressed an urge to scream at the top of my voice and my hands struggled against my reason in an attempt to break free and tear these harsh fingers holding the stethoscope away from the child's chest. But I stood there with my mouth shut and my hands still; for my reason remained alert and strong and true to science; and the god of science is mighty and merciless...

★ ★ ★ ★

He stood in front of me with his bare legs twisted and covered in thick hair. He looked at me in protest: 'Shall I take off my underpants too?'

The professor looked back at him coldly and unrelentingly and ordered, 'Take off all your clothes!'

The sick man went on looking at me in consternation and hesitantly took hold of the waistband of his pants. Allowing him no respite, the professor strode forward and pulled them down, leaving the man stark naked before us.

I put on the sterile gloves and advanced towards him. He fidgeted in embarrassment and irritation... How could a woman make him undress and then examine him? He tried hard to back away but the professor slapped his face hard, after which he submitted to my probing fingers as if he were a corpse.

The god of science knows no mercy and no shame. How harsh he was! How much I suffered in my worship of him! The body of a living person lost all respect and dignity and became exactly like a dead body under my gaze and my searching fingers, and disintegrated in my mind into a jumble of organs and dismembered limbs.

★ ★ ★ ★

The night was cold and desolate, the darkness dead and still. The great hospital with its lighted windows crouched in the dark like a wild hyena. The patients' groans and racking coughs tore at the curtains of the night. I stood alone at the window of my room, staring at the little white flower opening in the vase beside me. As I touched it I shuddered as if I was a corpse touching a living thing for the first time. I brought it close to my face and inhaled its perfume, feeling like a condemned prisoner pressing his nose against the iron bars of his cell to breathe in the fragrance of life. I put my hand up to my neck and my fingers brushed the metal arms of the stethoscope encircling my neck like a hangman's noose. The white coat hung round my shoulders reeking of ether, disinfectant and iodine.

What had I done to myself? Bound my life to illness, pain and death; made my daily occupation the uncovering of people's bodies so that I could see their private parts, feel their swollen sores and analyse their secretions. I no longer saw anything of life except sick people lying in their beds dazed, weeping or unconscious; their eyes dull, yellow or red; their limbs paralysed or amputated; their breathing irregular; their voices hoarse or groaning in pain. Could I bear this life sentence for the rest of my days? I felt a deep gloom like a prisoner must feel when his last flicker of hope has disappeared.

I left my room and went to sit in the big common room. I opened a medical journal and tried to read it, but I couldn't help my thoughts straying to the doctors' wing where the colleague on night duty was now asleep. For no obvious reason it occurred to me that I was alone with a man in the middle of the night and only a closed door separated me from him. Although I was wide awake this idea came to me like a dream and I felt afraid... No, not afraid, worried... No, not even that, for I felt desire, or not quite desire but a strange disturbing feeling that made me glance furtively at the closed door from time to time.

★ ★ ★ ★

The telephone buzzed at my elbow and the night sister's voice summoned me to a woman patient's bedside. I was there in a flash. She was a young married woman. I listened to her heartbeat; the valves had thickened with rheumatism and begun to make discordant noises, unlike the melodies I'd heard before from healthy hearts. The valves had lost their suppleness and could no longer shut the doors of the heart tightly, so that the blood seeped through them with a gurgling noise like that of a rotten water-wheel.

I looked at the young woman and saw a gleam in her eyes. 'What shall I call him?' she asked me. 'He's my first child.'

I gave her an injection, hiding her eyes from my sight behind a veil of anaesthetic, and said, 'I don't know. We don't yet know if it'll be a boy or a girl.'

Time passed, terrible moments, and I watched the child's smooth black head emerge from the darkness into the light, enclosed by the hard metallic jaws of science. I listened to the woman's heart struggling and groaning, the blood gurgling weakly and the valves thumping away strenuously. Then the child shot out and uttered a loud cry and I beamed in jubilation, taken aback at the sight of this human being opening his tiny eyes on life for the first time and seeing the big wide world.

The next moment I became aware of a terrible silence like the silence of the tomb. The gurgle of blood and the thumping of the valves had ceased. I looked at the woman; her face was as cold and still as a granite statue and her chest immobile like a wooden box. What had happened to her? A few moments before she'd been talking, moving and breathing. I rushed to use all the resources known to medical science for snatching human life from the claws of death. I injected her veins with solutions and stimulants; forced oxygen up her nose; tried artificial respiration to get her lungs working; stuck a long needle directly into her heart; opened her chest and began to massage her heart to restore life to it; blew into her mouth and slapped her face to try and get a reaction out of her. But nothing worked. Science was impotent. Nothing on earth had the power to raise this little closed eyelid even one more time.

I turned my attention to the newborn baby, kicking its legs and crying and screaming in the nurse's arms. Wasn't it extraordinary that this lump of live flesh had come out of that stiff dead body lying on the cold metal table? I buried my head in my hands and sat down heavily in a nearby chair. Why was science, the tyrannical god to whom I'd made obeisance, incapable of explaining to me how the valves in the heart could be destroyed by the effects of rheumatism? How could a young woman's heart stop for ever? How could a dying woman give birth to a living child, a tiny spark of life emerge from dead matter? How did the flame of life burn brightly and then go out? Whence does man come and whither does he go?

The focus of the struggle inside me widened out from masculinity and femininity to embrace humankind as a whole. Human beings appeared to be insignificant creatures in spite of their muscles, their brain cells and the complexity of their arterial and nervous systems. A small microbe, invisible to the naked eye, could be breathed in through the nose and eat away at the cells of the lungs. An unidentifiable virus could strike at random and make the cells of the liver or spleen or any other part of the body multiply at a crazy rate and devour everything around them. A small sticky drop that found its way from the tonsils to the heart could result in paralysis. The jab of a fine needle in the tiniest finger could take away hearing, sight and speech. One random air bubble could infiltrate the bloodstream by accident and the body would become a motionless corpse like a stinking, putrefying dog or horse.

This arrogant, proud and mighty man, constantly strutting and fretting, thinking and innovating, was supported on earth by a body separated from extinction by a hair's breadth. Once severed — and severed it must inevitably be one day — there was no power on earth which could join it together again.

Science toppled from its throne and fell at my feet naked and powerless, just as man had done before.

I looked around me, confused and upset: science had destroyed my former belief without leading me to any new faith. I realized that the path of reason which I had pledged to follow was a short, shallow one ending at a huge, impenetrable barrier.

I opened my eyes wide. What should I do? Retrace my steps or nestle up to the obstruction and cling to it for protection? Neither choice was really open to me: my acts of rebellion had given me a sort of strength and willpower which made it impossible for me to cling to anything outside myself for protection, the more so if that thing was a huge obstacle with no way through it.

So I found my feet taking me in a completely new direction.

3

I packed my few belongings and boarded the train that was to carry me far away from the city... away from the science professors and their laboratories, from my mother and the rest of my family, and from men and women alike.

In a remote, peaceful village I took a little house. I sat on the balcony of my country abode, shifting my gaze from the wide, peaceful green fields to the clear blue sky. The sun's warm rays fell on my body as I sprawled on a comfortable couch. I stretched and yawned in delicious indolence.

For the first time there was nobody else with me, and I felt as if I was divesting myself of the covering layers which had accumulated over the long years of my past life. I was confronted by my naked self and I began to examine what I saw in minute detail.

I didn't take a knife in my hand or put a stethoscope to my ear, but I stripped myself bare of the medical and scientific knowledge I'd acquired, the people I'd seen and known, and the battles I'd lived through over the years, which had finally led me up a blind alley in my thinking. I unloaded my thoughts as well, and began to feel.

For the first time in my life I was feeling without thinking, feeling the warm sun on my body, feeling that beautiful placid greenness which clothed the earth, the enchanting deep blue covering the sky. Face to face with nature, I saw its enchanting magic unspoilt by the hollow clamour of the city; the debased, imprisoned womanliness of woman; the arrogant overbearing masculinity of man; and the limited, ineffectual chatter of science.

I realized that nature was a beautiful and mighty god which frail, proud humanity in its brief lifetime had tried to clothe in cheap, ugly garments merely for the sake of pride and a sense of achievement. I felt my heart beating faster and this filled my spirit with strange currents of sentiments and emotions. For the first time for ages I could feel my heart beating without my mind racing ahead to draw mental pictures of heart muscles and arteries and estimate the amount of blood pouring from it. There was a new language to my heartbeats which neither science nor medicine could have explained, a language I understood with my newly awakened feelings but which would have been incomprehensible to my old experienced mind. I felt that emotion was sharper-witted than reason. It was more deeply rooted in the human heart, more firmly bound to the distant history of the human race, truer and more responsive to its nature and thoroughly proven by its experience.

I stretched out further on the couch, flexing my

legs and abandoning myself to the new rush of emotions which swept through my body. A sudden thought occurred to me: this was the body I'd once sentenced to death, the female body I'd mercilessly sacrificed at the feet of the god of science and reason, and it was coming to life again. I'd wasted my childhood and adolescence and the dawn of my young womanhood in a fierce battle: against whom? Against myself, my humanity and my natural impulses. And for no reason, since I was about to leave it all behind and begin afresh, start from the cradle of life, with the primitive flat land which yielded crops with spontaneous benevolence; with virgin nature which had covered the earth for millions of years; with the simple country people who ate the fruits of the earth and followed their instincts under a canopy of trees, and ate, drank, bore children, sickened and died without ever asking how or why.

I smiled, then laughed out loud so that I could hear myself laughing. My mother had always told me that a girl shouldn't laugh loud enough for people to hear, so my laughter had always faded on my lips before it made a sound. I opened my mouth as wide as it would go and laughed and snorted and the air flooded into my chest — pure, clean air free of smoke and carbon monoxide... and free of medical science and all the refinements of society. The composition of this air didn't concern me; I just knew that it was refreshing and cooled my overheated insides. I abandoned myself to the sun's rays and let them fall on my body — pure, clean rays unspoilt by scientific analyses of their properties, whether harmful or beneficial.

A simple, good-natured countryman brought me a tray of food: flat bread, cream, butter and eggs. I ate with a zest that I hadn't felt since I was a small child of under nine. I forgot my mother's instructions about how a girl should eat, and the medical profession's warnings about butter and cream, and stuffed my mouth with food. I drank cold water from an earthenware jug, making a loud noise and spilling water all down my clothes. I ate till my hunger was satisfied and drank till my thirst was quenched. The couch was scorching hot by now so I went and stretched out on the cool damp earth. I rested my face against it, drawing into me the smell that came from deep inside, and exulting in the sensation of belonging to it and being a part of it.

A gentle breeze lifted my skirt up over my thighs but I felt none of the alarm that I would have done in the past whenever my thighs were uncovered. How had my mother managed to instil in me this notion that my body was somehow shameful? Man was born naked and he died naked. All his clothes were a mere pretence, an attempt to cover up his true nature.

As I let the breeze lift up my clothes, I felt that I had been reborn, and that only at the instant of this rebirth had my emotional life properly come into being. But although newborn, it was a mighty giant, wanting to live... indeed, demanding its right to live.

★ ★ ★ ★

I was woken in the middle of the night by the sound of heavy knocking at the door. I looked out and saw a sick old man supported by a group of peasants. I let them in, put on my white coat and sounded the sick man's chest. The sound of his heartbeats was mixed with the sound of groaning and I raised my eyes to look at him. His eyes were fixed desperately on me like a drowning man staring at a lifebelt just out of his reach. It was as if I had suddenly forgotten all knowledge and had never examined a patient before. For the first time I was really seeing the eyes of a person suffering and hearing the sound of his groans.

How had I been able to examine patients in the past? How had my teachers led me to believe that a sick person was nothing more than a liver, a spleen or a collection of guts and entrails? How had they made me look into people's eyes, shine my light into them, turn up the lids with my fingers, without noticing their freshness and innocence? How had they made me look down people's throats without hearing their cries of pain?

I shuddered. For the first time in my life I was seeing the patient as a whole person, not a loose assemblage of discrete parts. The weariness and sickness of the old man's eyes were getting through to me and his cries were crossing the gap between my ears and my heart.

I stood at a loss before my patient, my eyes firmly on his, my ears-straining to pick up his faint whispered moaning, my soul dumbly watching the unfamiliar scene of human suffering, my mind silently taking in a new meaning to life.

I rested my hand on my heart and leant my head against the wall. There was something profoundly disturbing in the dull, despairing eyes. Something in the faint moaning made my spirit quail. It was an unfamiliar thing which I hadn't recognized before, been aware of or suffered from: pain, yes, pain! For the first time in my life I was feeling pain. It was a deep feeling which penetrated many layers and reached far inside me until it arrived at the centres of pleasure. I was in pain but I felt the pleasure of pain, the pleasure of my humanity as I exercised its redundant powers and investigated its unfamiliar horizons.

My whole being drank this pleasure to the lees, and my soul sucked the sensation of pain dry. This made me feel dizzy and I fell back into a nearby chair, shut my eyes and began to cry. I cried as I had never cried before, as if my eyes had never known what it was to cry. Stinging tears, always held back before, rained down my cheeks in a stormy torrent and I made no attempt to curb them. Let them come for all they were worth to wash my mind clean of its accumulated dust, to dislodge the dark veil that was insulating my heart, and to set my soul free from the prison cell of deadly rigidity where it languished! I gave in to the pain.

I came to my senses when I heard a sound; it was a weak sound, but full of warmth. I heard him saying, 'Don't cry, doctor. I'm all right.'

I opened my eyes and looked at him. His smile was faint and composed, but it betrayed affection and kindness. It was as if he was the one who felt compassion for me, wanted to take me by the hand and give me of what he had; as if he was the one who possessed knowledge and strength while I possessed nothing. A physical illness seemed to dwindle to nothing when compared with a spiritual illness. I felt that he was the doctor and I the patient.

I wouldn't have believed that my faith in humanity would revive just when I'd lost it and decided that human life had less substance than a bubble of air... nor that when I'd lost it amidst the bright lights of the city with all its glittering buildings, aeroplanes and advanced weaponry, I'd recover it in a benighted cave... and at the hands of a sick old countryman who owned nothing but the clothes he stood up in, rather than among professors of medicine and intellectuals.

It was a little smile from dry, cracked lips but it contained the meaning of life... that meaning which is lost to people in the crowd, which science loses sight of amid the clamour of its apparatus, and which reason is incapable of explaining. That meaning was love — a love of life and all its pleasure and pain, in sickness and in health, the known and unknown parts of it, the beginnings and the endings. Love. My heart pounded at the new word, a tremor of longing went through me and a fire was kindled within me.

★ ★ ★ ★

How could I go on living? I was at one and the same time an eager child with unspoilt, untried feelings and

47

a qualified doctor with an old mind. Twenty-five years of my life had passed without my feeling what it was to be a woman. My heart hadn't once beaten faster because of a man, nor had my lips tasted that wondrous thing known as a kiss. I hadn't passed through the glowing heat of adolescence. My childhood had been wasted fighting against my mother, my brother and myself. Textbooks had consumed my adolescence and the dawn of my womanhood. And so here I was, a child of twenty-five wanting to play, run, fly and love.

★ ★ ★ ★

I gathered together my few belongings and boarded the train which was to carry me out into the world and away from myself. I'd become acquainted with my self: I no longer needed to cling so strongly to it that I was cut off from life. Life, the essence of which I'd gathered from the earth like a pigeon picking up grain in its beak; life, which I'd begun to love with every cell of my being, body and soul, and which I felt an overwhelming desire to hold on to.

After all that had happened how could I shut myself away in dreary isolation? I had to go back; so I returned to my home, my family, my work and my patients. I opened my arms to life and embraced my mother, feeling for the first time that she was my mother. I embraced my father and understood what it meant to be a daughter, and embraced my brother and knew the feeling of brotherly love. Then I looked around me, searching for something that was still missing, someone who wasn't there. Who was it? My depths cried out for him, my soul called to him. Who could he be?

A violent longing swept through me, my body and soul — the yearning of a soul thirsty for love and set free by reason, and of a virginal body newly let out of its iron cell. I wondered what an encounter between a man and a woman was like. The nights grew longer as the fantasies and illusions gathered round my bed. Long powerful arms encircled my waist. A man's face came closer to mine. He had eyes like my father's and a mouth like my cousin's, but he wasn't either of them. Who was he? The chatter of the girls at school floated to the surface of my memory. I sighed and moaned and had the fantasies of an adolescent girl; it was as if I'd never dissected a man's body or stripped it naked and been repelled by its ugliness.

Had I forgotten... ? I don't know... But I had forgotten... And now the mystery and wonder of the living human body was restored for me... Perhaps my womanhood had emerged defiantly from its prison, dismantling on its way all the memories stored in my mind. Perhaps the stormy yearnings of my soul had uprooted the ugly images of the body from my imagination, or the violent trembling of my heart had dislodged the knowledge of medical science from my head.

Dawn no longer broke. The warmth of my bed turned into a blazing furnace and the morning light could do nothing to scatter the dreams of the night.

4

The telephone shrilled next to my bed and I half opened an eye to look at the time. It was two in the morning. Sluggishly I picked up the receiver and an urgent voice said to me: 'Doctor! My mother's very ill. Please come and save her.'

I jumped out of the warm bed, hurriedly pulled on my coat, snatched up the little case that stood ready for emergency calls and drove at speed to the patient's house.

I listened to her fading heartbeat, the sound of a heart weakened through old age, and from which life was about to slip away. I took the stethoscope away from my ears and looked about me, registering the presence of a tall man standing near me with a look of desperate anxiety in his eyes: 'Is she very bad, doctor?'

I went out of the room without replying. He followed me into the living-room and asked me again impatiently, 'Is it very serious?'

'No,' I said slowly, 'it's nothing serious. She's just dying.'

He stared at me in horror and amazement and said,

'Dying? No! That's impossible!'

He buried his head in his hands, flung himself into a nearby chair and began to cry with a stifled, shuddering sound. I waited till his fit of sobbing had passed and he lifted his eyes to look at me, then I said to him, 'Everybody has to die.'

'But she's my mother, doctor.'

'Old age has caught up with her. It's quite normal for her to die now.'

He wiped his eyes and I reached out my hand to shake his, saying, 'Let her stay in her own room so that she can end her life in peace.'

Tears welled up in his eyes again and I opened the door and went out.

★ ★ ★ ★

I was sitting in my office with a glass of warm aniseed in my hand — the duty nurse had made it for me as the last patient left the surgery. My tired fingers curled around the glass seeking comfort and relaxation in its warmth. I brought my weary face close to the steam rising from it, inhaling deeply, for I liked the smell of aniseed more than its taste. At that moment the nurse came in and announced that there was a man who wanted to see me.

The man came in. I recognized him and stood up to shake his hand. As he sat down opposite, I noticed that he was wearing a black tie. I offered him my condolences. 'Thank you, doctor,' he replied, looking down.

He remained with his head bowed and I picked up my glass of aniseed and took a long drink from it. He raised his eyes and looked curiously at the glass.

'Would you like a glass of aniseed?' I asked him.

He looked at me in surprise: 'Aniseed?'

I laughed at his surprise, and he smiled and said, 'I came to thank you.'

'I didn't do anything.'

'You came out in the middle of the night.'

'That's a doctor's job.'

'You told me the truth.'

'I wouldn't have kept it from you in this case.'

'It's a very painful thing.'

I didn't answer and he looked at me and said, 'Don't you find it painful to look at a person who's dying?'

'It's the most bearable form of pain that I come across.'

'What's harder to accept than death?'

'An incurable illness or severe physical deformity or mental deficiency.'

'Have you had to see all these things?'

'They're part of every doctor's life.'

'Forgive me, doctor. I don't deal with vulnerable human beings in my work. I handle solid rock.'

'Are you an engineer?'

'Yes.'

We were both silent for a moment, then I said to him, 'But have you never known pain and suffering in your life?'

'That's the first time I've seen someone dying and

the first time I've cried since I was a tiny child.'

This amazed me. Life was hard, much harder than rock! 'So you haven't experienced life yet,' I said.

He looked me in the eye and seemed about to say something but then decided against it. I thought I saw a strange expression in his eyes: an expression of weakness and need mixed with childishness and naivety, which made me eager to do something for him. He stood up and stretched out his hand saying, 'Thanks again, doctor.'

He turned and made for the door but didn't go out immediately. He looked back at me, apparently struggling to get some words out. Then I heard him say, 'I'd like to talk to you again some time, but... '

He stopped then began again, not looking anywhere near me: 'I know you don't have much spare time.'

I didn't answer and, still averting his eyes from me, he stammered out, 'Can I see you again?'

I stared into his face: there was a look in his eyes which caught my attention, but his expression didn't convince me; the only death he had seen was his mother's, and he was unfamiliar with illness and pain. Would he be able to satisfy this old experienced mind or excite the interest of this greedy and totally unrestrained child?

But he was the first man my eyes had rested on, and I said, 'You can see me again.'

★ ★ ★ ★

I sat beside him on one of the big stones forming the base of the pyramid, straining my eyes to the distant horizon and watching the sun's red disc as it crept out from behind thick grey clouds.

'What are you thinking about, doctor?' I heard him saying.

'Why do you always call me doctor?'

'Don't you like it?'

'It reminds me of my patients calling me when they're in pain.'

'It's a magical title. I feel proud to use it when I'm talking to you. You're the first woman doctor I've known.'

'Really?'

'When I sent for you to come and see my mother, I didn't think I was talking to the doctor when I heard your voice on the phone. And when I saw you coming into my mother's room I couldn't believe you were the doctor.'

'Why not?'

'I'd imagined that a woman doctor would be ugly or old or both, with thick glasses and a bent back from so much reading and hard work. It hadn't occurred to me that she might be a beautiful woman.'

'Why not?'

'It's difficult for a woman to combine being beautiful with being clever.'

'Why?'

'I don't know.'

'Then I'll tell you: because from early childhood a girl is brought up to believe that she's a body and nothing more, so her body becomes her main concern for the rest of her life, and she doesn't realize that she's got a mind as well which must be looked after and encouraged to develop.'

'Why do they do that?'

[...] who hold the key positions in life, [...] to be anything more than beauti- [...]s whose legs they can lie between [...]ke it. Men don't want women as [...], they want them to be subordinate and to serve them.'

He laughed and so did I. He came closer and said, 'I'm not one of those men. I want a woman who's my partner, not my servant. I'm proud of your mind. [...] hen I go into [...] all those men [...] em and make [...] ion and your [...] a mind like [...] king? Or one [...] vaste her life — or worse, [...], an insult to

[...] ny rebellious [...] rt. I felt the [...] porating and [...] inst the stone [...] spoken to me like this, or society recognized the truth of notions such as these? And here was a man doing it, acknowledging that women had minds; that a woman, just like a man, had both a body and a mind. Here was a man uttering the very words I'd said to myself ever since I'd first noticed what was going on around me.

I looked at him, trying to make out where these just, mature words were coming from. From the hidden depths of him or from his throat? I could see nothing. The gap between his depths and his throat was non-existent. Perhaps I didn't see any depth to him, or perhaps the sun had dropped into that deep chasm into which it vanishes every night and the shadows had blurred the sharp outlines of things.

I felt his cold hands and looked into his face. His gentle, submissive smile aroused my maternal instincts, but his weak, beseeching glances failed to arouse my femininity. Was it because he was weak, weaker than me? Or because he hadn't my experience of suffering? Or because his eyes lacked that profound inner strength which I thought a man's eyes should possess? Could it be because I still had in my blood the instincts of a wild woman of the forest who loved the man who made her submit to him? But he appealed to something in me. Perhaps his weakness gave me the confirmation of my own strength. Perhaps the look of need in his eyes was gratifying to my mind which still wanted to dominate.

★ ★ ★ ★

Smiling, he said to me, 'Mummy had the same strong expression... but her eyes were green.'

57

The word 'mummy' sounded out-of-place and incongruous coming out from under a thick bushy moustache which made his features look like those of a small child with a dead black insect stuck to its upper lip.

'Why are you looking at me like that?' I heard him say.

'Did you love your mother?'

His eyes filled with tears for a moment. 'Very much,' he said. I was unmoved by his tears. He went on, 'After she died, the world seemed empty... but I found you and it was full again.'

'That's strange!'

'What is?'

'That the world can seem empty to you after someone's died.'

'She was my mother, and I loved her tremendously. Everything she did was for my sake. What about you? Didn't you love your mother?'

'I loved her... but she never filled my life.'

'Perhaps you loved your father more?'

'No more, no less.'

'So who was the most important person in your life?'

'It wasn't a person.'

'What was it?'

'I don't know. Maybe my life's never been full. Or maybe I was trying to achieve something.'

'What kind of thing?'

'I don't know. Perhaps some great undertaking.'

'Making people better?'

'Maybe something more than that.'

★ ★ ★ ★

'Would you like to live with me for ever?'

He asked me this, looking at me like a motherless child. He aroused powerful maternal, humanitarian and altruistic instincts and desires in me, and I felt his need for me pulling me towards him and binding me to him.

I looked at him tenderly and he asked me again, 'Will you marry me?'

The word 'marry' thudded inside my head, driving all other thoughts to the back of my mind. What had it meant to me when I was a child? A man with a big belly. In my mind, the smell of the kitchen was the smell of marriage. I hated the word and I hated the smell of food. Without realizing what I was doing, I asked him, 'Do you like food?'

He looked at me in surprise and said, 'Food?'

'Yes.'

'What strange question are you asking me this time?'

'Men get married to eat.'

'Who told you that?'

'Everybody.'

'It's not true.'

'Why didn't you think about getting married while your mother was living with you?'

'My mother didn't just cook for me. She gave me everything else I wanted.'

'So you're getting married so that someone else can

give you everything you want?'

'No,' he said; and it was as if he was saying, 'Yes.'

★ ★ ★ ★

The old man with a large white turban looked at him with profound respect and listened to everything he said, but he didn't see or hear me. I seemed to vanish before his eyes. He had a pen in his hand and there was a big lined exercise book on the table in front of him.

'How much do you wish to pay in advance, sir, and what will the balance be?'

What were these melancholy phrases coming out of his dry lips? Advance? Balance? Was the man who had nothing to give me now paying so that he could marry me? But the man in the turban had no way of knowing which of us was the one with something to give. All he saw was a man and a woman and as far as he was concerned the man was the one with the possessions.

I looked at the shaikh with a superior expression and said, 'Write "nothing".'

He looked back at me disapprovingly: how dare a woman speak in the presence of men!

'The contract then becomes invalid,' he pronounced in a legalistic tone.

'Why?'

'The law tells us so.'

'Then you don't know the law.'

He jumped up from his chair and his turban bounced off his head. He caught it in both hands, shouting, 'God have mercy! God have mercy!'

★ ★ ★ ★

The shaikh moistened his fingers with the tip of his tongue, plunged the pen into the ink, muttered the appropriate religious formulae, pushed back his voluminous sleeve, then wrote out two forms and handed me one of them, saying 'Sign here.'

Stubbornly I replied, 'Let me read it through first.'

He looked at me irritably but gave me the paper to read. My eyes fell on unexpected words, words that I associated with contracts for renting flats and shops and plots of agricultural land: 'On this day... in my presence and by my hand... I so-and-so... official attached to such-and-such a court... marriage of so-and-so to so-and-so... on payment of such-and-such a marriage portion by the husband... an amount to be paid at the present time... and an amount to be deferred... legal marriage according to God's Book and the Law of His Prophet, God bless Him and grant Him salvation... with the legal consent of the afore-mentioned husband... consequent on both parties being verified as free from any religious or civil impediment and on the wife having no income or salary from the government and no wealth exceeding... in the presence of the witnesses...'

I took the document in both hands, ready to tear it into shreds, but my husband-to-be took it from me, and the weakness and need that I saw in his eyes made me feel ashamed of my act of rebellion and despise myself for going against him. He said quietly, 'It's just a formality; nothing more,' and I signed.

★ ★ ★ ★

I might as well have signed my death warrant. My name, the first word I ever heard and which was linked in my conscious and subconscious mind with my existence and very being, became null and void. He attached his name to the outside of me. I sat at his side, hearing people call me by my new name. I looked at them and at myself in astonishment as if they couldn't really be addressing me. It was as if I'd died and my spirit had passed into the body of another woman who looked like me but had a strange new name.

My private world, my bedroom, was no longer mine alone. My bed, which no one had ever shared before, became his too. Every time I turned over or moved, my hand came into contact with his rough tousled head or his arm or leg, sticky with sweat. The sound of his breathing beside me filled the air round about with a mournful lament. Nothing bound me to this man when his eyes were closed. I saw him as a lifeless body like the ones in the dissecting room. But whenever he opened his eyes and gave me one of his weak, pleading glances which aroused my maternal instincts but failed to arouse any sexual response in me, I saw him as my own child, sprung from my loins in a place and at a time of which I had no recollection.

✱ ✱ ✱ ✱

I'm ... you ... 63 *continues.. Husband tries get in the way of work...*

'I'm the man.'

'So what?'

'I'm in charge.'

'In charge of what?'

'Of this house and all that's in it, including you.'

The first signs of rebellion were showing themselves: his feeling of weakness in front of me had been translated inside him into a desire to control me.

'I don't want you going out every day,' he said.

'I don't go out for fun. I work.'

'I don't want you examining men's bodies and undressing them.'

The weak spot that a man focuses on in his attempt to gain control over a woman: her need to be protected from other men. The male's jealousy over his female: he claims to be frightened for her when he's really frightened for himself, claims to be protecting her in order to take possession of her and put four walls around her.

'We don't need the income from the practice,' he insisted.

'I don't work for money. I love my work.'

'You need to be free for your husband and your home.'

'What do you mean?'

'Close the practice.'

He'd reached the conclusion that it was my work which endowed me with the strength that prevented him controlling me. He thought that the money I earnt each month, however much or little it was, was what made me hold my head up high. He didn't realize that my strength wasn't because I had a job, nor was my pride because I had my own income, but both were because I didn't have the psychological need for him that he did for me. I didn't have this need for my mother, my father or anyone else because I wasn't dependent on anyone, whereas he'd been dependent on his mother, then had begun to replace her with me.

And yet he considered himself a man. He had a man's features: a deep voice and a bushy moustache. Other men were in his employ, women stole glances at his moustache and children he passed in streets and alleys didn't dare make rude remarks or throw stones at him.

★ ★ ★ ★

'Close down the practice,' he insisted.

'What about the patients, and all the people I'd be letting down?'

'There are other doctors besides you.'

'And my future, and the knowledge I've spent half my life acquiring?'

'I'm your life.'

'And all those things you said to me?'

'I didn't know what it would be like.'

I looked at him with my eyes wide open. His eyes were pale and without depth. His hands were hard and rougher than I'd pictured, his fingers shorter and stupid-looking. Who was this stranger beside me? Who was this lump of flesh I called my husband?

He moved close to me, took my hand, whispered in my ear and put his face against mine. I tried to forget his self-important look and the inconsistency of what he said, tried to deny the evidence of my ears and eyes, but it was impossible. My memory was clear and vigilant, retaining every word. My mind was all too alert, forcing me to face images of the depressing reality of him. I could see right up close to me his teeth and his big flat rabbit's ears.

I drew away but he put his sweaty arms around me, whispering in my ear in a hoarse, sad voice. I pushed him off me in annoyance and said angrily, 'Why did you lie to me?'

'I wanted to have you.'

'That's ridiculous. I'm not a piece of land!'

'I'm the one who gives the orders! I'm your husband!'

The look of weakness and need was gone from his eyes and the thread that had been binding me to him was severed. A hard, overbearing expression rose to the surface of his shallow eyes: not the look of a strong man, but of a weak man when he develops an inferiority complex because he's used to seeing himself as the strong one out in the streets and senses that he's the weak one inside his own home.

★ ★ ★ ★

I sat in my surgery with my head in my hands and

admitted to myself that I'd made a mistake. I'd believed a man's words in the dark without being able to see into the depths of him. I'd been seduced by his weakness and his wanting me. I hadn't realized that a weak person conceals complexes and mean, contemptible characteristics under the surface which someone stronger would scorn and rise above. Yes, I'd done wrong. I'd disobeyed my heart and mind and done what this man wanted, entered into a marriage contract which looked like a contract for renting a shop or a flat. By doing that hadn't I put him in authority over me? Hadn't this contract made him my husband?

My husband! These words I'd never spoken before! What did they mean to me? A hefty body, taking up half the bed. A gaping mouth which never stopped eating. Two flat feet which dirtied socks and sheets. A thick nose which kept me awake all night long with its snorting and whistling.

What should I do now? Accept responsibility for my mistake and put up with living with him for ever? But how could I live with him, talk to him, look into his eyes, give him my lips, degrade my body and soul with him? No, no. The wrong I'd done didn't deserve all this punishment; it didn't.

Everybody does wrong. Life is made up of right and wrong. We only come to know what's right through our mistakes. It's not weak and stupid to do wrong, but to continue doing wrong.

★ ★ ★ ★

People opened their mouths wide in astonishment and protest. How could she leave her husband? And why?

How dare they, these people who handed themselves over to me body and soul, whom I saved from ruinous illness and death? What right had they to object to something in my private life, or to tell me their opinions? I was the one who advised them what to eat and drink, explained to them how to breathe, sleep, live, multiply... Had they forgotten, or did they think that when I took off my stethoscope and white coat, I put aside my mind and intelligence and personality? How little they knew!

My mother had ruined my childhood, learning had swallowed up my adolescence and early womanhood and the years left to me of my youth could be counted on the fingers of one hand. I wasn't going to waste them and no one was going to make me.

5

The little world that I used to build out of chairs and dolls when I was a child became reality. In my pocket was the magic key. I could come and go whenever I wanted without having to ask anyone's permission. I slept alone in a bed without a husband, turning over from right to left or from left to right as I fancied. I sat at my desk to read and write or to ponder and think or do nothing at all.

I was free, completely free in this little world of mine. I shut my door and cast off my artificial life with other people along with my shoes and clothes, and I pottered around the house at will. I was completely alone there. I couldn't hear voices or people breathing and I didn't have to look at other people's bodies. For the first time in my life a heavy burden was lifted from my heart, the burden of living in a house shared by others.

★ ★ ★ ★

In the middle of the night I opened my eyes to the

sound of the heartbeats thudding in my chest like the weary marching feet of a defeated army. My breathing grated beneath my ribs with a noise like the squeaking of a worn-out water-wheel. My open eyes saw only blackness, and my ears drummed in the terrible deadly silence. I was frightened that my heart would stop creeping along, my breathing grate to a halt, the darkness quench the light of my eyes and my hearing be lost amid the drumming.

I stared into the darkness, testing out my sight, and strained my ears. I saw the big mass of blackness splitting up into lots of smaller masses with heads and tails and horns, and sounds spread into the dead silence: whispering, rustling, wailing. I buried my head under the covers and the apparitions and noises vanished. The thudding in my chest abated and the squeaking noise died away. The warmth of the bed coursed into my joints and along my limbs and I yawned contentedly, stretching out my arms, feeling for sleep. But sleep wasn't there, and I took something else in my arms, or someone — someone who had eyes like my father but wasn't my father, and lips like my cousin but wasn't my cousin. Who was he? The spectre which had haunted the nights of my youth began to visit me again. The nights grew longer and the bed wider. Solitude no longer seemed so attractive.

★ ★ ★ ★

Where would I find him? How in this vast crowded

world could I hope to come across the insubstantial being so familiar to my inner self, the spectre of a man lodged firmly in my imagination? I knew the look in his eyes, the timbre of his voice, the shape of his fingers, the warmth of his breath, the depths of his heart and mind. I knew, I knew. I can't tell how, but I knew.

Did he exist in real life or was he entirely a figment of my imagination? Would I meet him one day or go on waiting for him for ever? And what about this giant longing to love and be loved which lay dormant inside me? Should I exclude it from my life or try to satisfy it? But how could I satisfy it when it preferred total deprivation to spurious or incomplete satisfaction? I wanted a perfect man like the one in my imagination and a perfect love and I wasn't going to abandon either of these goals, however long it meant I had to be alone. 'All or nothing' was my abiding principle and I'd never accept half measures.

I decided to search for him everywhere: in palaces and caves, in night clubs and monasteries, in the factories of science and the temples of art, in bright lights and in pitch dark, on lofty summits and down deep chasms, in bustling cities and in wild deserted forests.

Why were people staring at me in amazement? Hadn't I wasted enough of my life to satisfy them? Did they want me to sit at home, chin in hand, waiting for some man to come and buy me like a cow? Wasn't it my natural right to choose my man? And how was I supposed to do it? By meeting only other women, or looking at pictures in books, or taking the only man who chose me? Obviously I had to look at lots of men to find him. I had to move around, looking at their faces and into their eyes, listening to their voices and the way they breathed, touching their fingers and their moustaches, examining their hearts and minds. How could I possibly recognize my man in the darkness or from behind a window blind or from a kilometre away? Wasn't it vital for me to see him in the light, try him out and get to know him? Didn't experience precede knowledge, or did they want me to go wrong like last time? I had no choice but to plunge without scruples into the most risky experience in a woman's life, choosing a man and looking for love.

★ ★ ★ ★

All I could see of him was his eyes. The rest of his face was always hidden behind a white protective mask and his fingers in sterile gloves. His body was concealed by the voluminous surgical gown and his feet by the surgical boots. His breath was lost in the pervasive smell of ether from the anaesthetizing equipment.

I saw him looking at me surreptitiously. We were alone in the room except for the unconscious man on the operating table whose eyes were closed and whose guts protruded from a large opening in his stomach. I wondered why he bothered to try and hide what he was doing: was he scared of the unconscious man or me or himself, or was it just his normal way of proceeding?

I heard him ask, 'Why are you so distracted? Who are you thinking about?'

'The man.'

'Which man?'

'The one whose stomach we've just opened up.'

He laughed, and I could hear it well enough, short and scornful, although I couldn't see his lips or his teeth. I was silent and he began fiddling around inside the man's stomach, feeling for his large intestine. After a bit he held it up in a pair of forceps and said, 'There's no point in removing it. The cancer's eaten into it and spread into the peritoneum.'

I looked at the sleeping man's face and felt as if a knife had been thrust into my chest. I looked down at the floor, silently swallowing back my tears.

I heard him laughing again and saying, 'Aren't you used to these things yet?'

'I'll never get used to them.'

He looked at me in silence and we stitched up the patient's stomach without another word until he said suddenly, 'Do you know who I'm thinking about?'

'No.'

'I'm thinking about you.'

He stressed every word, fixing his eyes on mine and instead of looking at the floor I looked carefully and deliberately back at him.

★ ★ ★ ★

He stared at me as if trying to convey all the notions of desire that it was possible for a man to have. 'Once a woman's been married, she's much more liberated than a young virgin.'

I looked at him angrily and said, 'My emancipation doesn't stem from a physical change within my body. And any restrictions on my body aren't because I fear for an insignificant hymen which can be torn by a random blow and restored by a surgeon's needle. I impose my own restrictions on myself voluntarily, and exercise my freedom, as I understand the word, in the same way.'

He glanced spitefully at me and said, 'Why are you scared then?'

'Scared of what?'

'Of me.'

'You!'

What did he want from me or what did I want from him? I wasn't sure, but I wanted to know something about men or about myself which was still unclear.

★ ★ ★ ★

I marched determinedly up to his front door and rang the bell with an air of confidence. He smiled broadly, not concealing his satisfaction at his victory, and said, 'I didn't think you'd come.'

'Why not?'

'I thought you didn't trust me yet.'

'I don't.'

I sat down and he came and sat next to me, his leg nearly touching mine. So I stood up and went to sit opposite. With a sly smile he asked, 'Why don't you want to sit beside me?'

Looking straight at him, I said, 'I prefer to sit facing you so that I can see your eyes.'

He didn't reply and I tried to force him to look at me but his eyes kept darting away. He thought for a moment then rose and went into another room and returned with a tall bottle. He filled a glass from it.

'What's that?' I asked.

'Your mind's as sharp as a sword.' He looked greedily at my legs. 'I want to escape from it.'

My mind was like a sword! He wanted to escape from my mind! Was this a battle? What did this man want? He had a strange smile, and as I studied his expression, I had the feeling that he was preparing himself for a battle he was determined to win. The battle between a man and a woman: that odd, artificial contest in which the woman faces the man alone, but the man stands barricaded by tradition, laws and creeds, backed up by generations and aeons of history, and row upon row of men, women and children, all with sharp tongues extended like the blades of a sword, eyes aimed like gun-barrels and mouths blazing away like machine-guns.

The man has the world supporting him and holds the sceptre of life in his hand. He owns the past, the present and the future. Honour, respect and morality are all his — decorations earned in the battle against women. He owns the spiritual and the material world. He even owns the drop of sperm planted in the woman at the end of the struggle. He chooses whether or not to acknowledge it, to grant it his name and an honourable place in life, to let it live or have it destroyed.

The woman stands before the man, deprived by the world of her freedom, her honour, her name, her self-respect, her true nature and her will. All control over her spiritual and material life has been taken from her, even her control over the little fruit which she creates inside her with her own blood and cells and the atoms of her mind and heart.

I saw him smiling again. Why are you smiling like that, Man? Would you be able to name this battle?

He moved up close to me, his hot breath stinging my face, and I backed away. He came after me on his hands and knees and I stood up and moved away from him.

What was going on? Why did a man crumble in the face of his desire? Why did his willpower vanish the minute he was shut in with a woman so that he turned into a wild animal on four legs? Where was his power? Where was his strength? Where were his authority and qualities of leadership? How weak men were! Why had my mother made gods of them?

I looked at him, at his eyes, his fingers and his toes. I turned the searchlight of my gaze on him and looked closely into the depths of his heart and mind only to find hollow, empty wastes, a shallow mind and a false heart. Then I knew why he wanted to free himself of my mind: he was like a thief wanting to steal something from me when I wasn't paying attention. I looked at him with pity and contempt. I felt sorry for him so I withdrew from the confrontation, despising myself for having considered a fight with someone so much weaker than me.

I felt stronger than him in spite of the barriers he dragged along with him, the barriers he surrounded himself with, the armoury supporting him. I didn't need any of this: my strength was inside me, in my being. I wouldn't let a man so much as touch my hand if I didn't want him to, even if I was shut up within four high walls with him; but if I wanted to, I would give him myself before the eyes of the world without secrecy or stealth. It was my will which guided my behaviour, not the place or the time or other people.

I saw him coming up to me again. He put his hand on mine and I felt an icy coldness steal over my soul. Nothing will work, Man, so take your hand off me. It feels quite out of place. My mind is convinced by my heart, and my body by my mind, and there is no way to persuade one of them independently of the others.

I reached for my bag and stood up.

'Are you going?' he asked in surprise.

'Yes.'

'Why?' His surprise grew.

What could I say to him? Why didn't he understand? Would he be able to believe me? Was it possible for a man to believe that there was a woman who could get inside him and see what he was hiding from her, or a woman who could make her body submit to the dictates of her heart and mind? A woman who could return his stare unblinking, remain unmoved when he touched her hand, be shut in a room with him and not give him a thing, and then leave him and go away saying, 'No. You're not the man I want.'

Could a man comprehend that a woman could take a good look at him and then reject him? He couldn't, because he was accustomed to being the only one with the right to experiment and choose, while the woman just had to accept whoever chose her: one special man, who spends his whole life convincing himself that he is this one special man. Isn't a woman just like a man, doctor? Have you forgotten your science? Or has your mind become separated from your body? Arrogance turns a man into a stupid, feeble-minded creature.

★ ★ ★ ★

Society impaled me with looks as sharp as daggers and lashed my face with stinging tongues like horse-whips.

How can a woman live alone without a man? Why is she going out? Why is she coming in? Why is she smiling? Why is she breathing? Why is she taking gulps of fresh air? Why is she looking at the moon? Why does she hold her head up and open her eyes wide? Why does she tread with confidence and pride? Isn't she embarrassed? Doesn't she want a man to protect her?

My family and relations attacked me. Even my closest friends vied with one another to discard me. I stood in the eye of the storm, thinking.

Since childhood I'd been immersed in a series of

endless battles and here I was up against a new one with society at large: millions of people, with millions more in front and behind. Why didn't things go as they ought to in life? Why wasn't there a greater understanding of truth and justice? Why didn't mothers recognize that daughters were like sons, or men acknowledge women as equals and partners? Why didn't society recognize a woman's right to lead a normal life using her mind as well as her body?

Why did they make me waste my life in these confrontations?

I rested my chin in my hands and sat thinking. Should I do battle with society or submit to it and be carried along by it, bowing my head to it, shutting myself up in my house and seeking protection from a man like all the rest?

No! Such thoughts were absurd. I would fight, looking to myself for protection, looking to my strength, my knowledge, my success in my work.

★ ★ ★ ★

I left everything behind: my family and friends; men and women; food and drink; sleeping and dreaming; the moon and the stars; wind and water. I put on my white coat, hung the stethoscope round my neck and stood in my surgery.

I'd decided to do battle, to drown in my own sweat, to face society on feet of iron.

★ ★ ★ ★

She came to see me in the surgery, her small body trembling with fear, panting, turning to look behind her, her innocent child's face contorted with terror.

'What's wrong, my girl?' I asked.

She shuddered as if she was feverish and started to sob her heart out. I managed to pick up a few disjointed, fragmented words from her quivering lips: 'He didn't do what he said... cruel bastard... Upper Egypt... they'll kill me... I haven't got anyone... save me, doctor.'

She didn't have a hanky, so I gave her mine and waited until she had no more tears left. She dried her eyes and fixed her frightened gaze on my lips, desperate to hear the one small word I would speak, granting her life or sentencing her to death.

I looked at her. She was a child of no more than fourteen or fifteen, innocent, pure, frail, with no income and no one to support her. I had no choice. How could I abandon her when I was all she had, or sentence her to death when I believed in her innocence and her right to life? How could I leave her neck under her father's knife when I knew that her father, mother, brother and uncle had all done wrong? How could I punish her alone when I knew that the whole of society had participated in the act, or wonder at her when I knew that everybody did similar things? How could I not protect her when she was the victim and society protected the real offender, or disapprove of her error when I myself had already fallen? I who had lived twice as long as her and seen and learnt many more things than she had. How could I not absolve her when I had already absolved myself?

I tried to save the poor child from the talons of the law and tradition and from the fangs of the wild beasts and the snakes, rats and cockroaches. I'd save her and they would crucify me if the idea appealed to them, stone me to death, take me to the scaffold. I'd accept my fate and meet death with a satisfied soul and an easy conscience.

★ ★ ★ ★

All society's tragedies came into my surgery. All the results of deception and deceit lay before me to be examined. The bitter truths which people constantly deny were stretched out on the operating table under my probing, cutting hands.

I felt compassion for people. Hadn't this man who'd butchered his erring sister done wrong himself with other men's sisters? Wasn't the wolf who'd deceived the innocent girl himself the father of a daughter whom he'd kept imprisoned in the house...? the man who'd been unfaithful to his wife also the husband who'd killed his wife to defend his honour...? the unfaithful wife the woman who spread rumours about other women...? this society which broadcast songs of love and passion the same society which erected the scaffold for all who fell in love or were swept away by passion?

I felt compassion for people, all people: they were both wrongdoers and the victims of wrongdoing.

★ ★ ★ ★

My surgery filled up with men, women and children and my coffers with money and gold. My name became as famous as that of a movie star and my opinions circulated among people as though they were law. Strangers suddenly claimed a relationship with me, enemies·became friends and confidants. Men swarmed round me like flies and their attacks changed into a defence of my position and gestures of support. The drawers of my desk filled up with testimonials, requests and pleas for help.

I sat on my lofty peak looking down on society at my feet. I smiled at it pityingly. Society — that mighty monster which seized women by the scruff of the neck and flung them into kitchens, abbatoirs, graves or the filthy mire — was lying in my desk drawers, weak, subdued and hypocritically begging for mercy! How small mighty society looked now!

I sat alone at my desk after the last patient had left and the duty nurse had gone home. It was still only nine in the evening, the beginning of the night, and the streets were at their liveliest. I stood up and began to pace the room distractedly. I went up to the window and the warm dreary night air touched my face. In the street outside, people were clinging to one another, talking, laughing, scowling. I looked at myself and found that I was looking down on them from a great height.

I felt a chilling cold as though I was sitting on a snowy mountain top. I looked above my head and saw only clouds and sky. I looked down at my feet and saw the great distance separating me from the soft gentle valleys and the low-lying plains warmed by the breath of humanity. I could see people waving at me from afar but no one climbed right up to where I was. They played tunes for me but the sounds didn't reach my ears. They threw flowers at me but the perfume vanished in the air.

I rested my forehead on the window-sill. How cold solitude was, how hard the silence! What should I do? Jump from the peak? But then I'd break my neck. Retrace my steps? But my life would pass and I'd never achieve what I wanted. My struggles were over and the time had come for me to sit doing nothing.

How terrible it was to have time lying on my hands!

Why had I bounded up the ladder of my profession instead of drinking from the cup of life sip by sip or savouring my time in small mouthfuls? Why had I jumped and panted over the course, leaving my proper place in the line and going over the heads of those in front of me?

People were moving along the street in their lines, advancing with all the speed of a tortoise, but they would arrive one day. Life was moving forward slowly but would inevitably get wherever it was going. Millions of years had gone by before atoms became air, and air became water and water became solid matter; and millions more had passed before the solid matter became moving amoebas, and the amoebas developed appendages, and they became fins, wings, arms and tails, and the arms grew fingers, and the tail became extinct and the ape stood upon two legs...

As a child, why had I been sad because I couldn't fly through the air like a pigeon? Why had I been angry at the blood which stains a woman every thirty days? Why had I rebelled against history and laws and tradition and raged because science hadn't discovered the secret of living protoplasm?

The years would go by and possibly time would transform history and laws and tradition. Life would discover a clean and beautiful way for little girls to mature. Human bodies would grow progressively lighter and fly. Science would stumble upon the secret of living protoplasm. The cavalcade of life moved along and each day life discovered something new. Why had time seemed so slow to me, its cogs tearing at parts of my life as it rumbled by? Why had life rushed me along and flung me away and up on to a lofty peak shrouded in icy loneliness?

How cruel the silence was and how gentle human voices, even if they were noisy. How cold the solitude and how warm the breathing of people, even the sick. How repellent inertia was and how beautiful movement, even struggle and conflict. How terrible empty time was, and how sweet thinking and being busy, even if the outcome was unsuccessful.

★ ★ ★ ★

The feeling of emptiness took root in me and the giant

found he had space to move. The throng of ideas and images inside me dispersed and the giant spread out his arms and legs and began lazily to yawn and stretch.

What do you want? You rebelled against everything and refused to lead a woman's life. You ran after truth and truth made you shut yourself away from yourself. And men? You looked at them, searched around and were thrown into disarray; then you pursed your lips disparagingly.

What do you want? A man who only exists in your imagination and doesn't walk about the earth? A man who talks, breathes and thinks but doesn't have a body like other men? Can you forget those bodies lying on the dissecting table, or the miserable sound of snoring near your pillow, or those despairing, helpless looks, or death which cuts children down? Why don't you shut yourself up in your prison cell and go back to sleep?

But the nights had grown long, and the nocturnal phantoms had taken up position around the bed again and the bed itself had become vast and cold and frightening. The giant didn't want to go back to sleep. Success didn't satisfy his hunger, fame was meaningless and money was just like dead withered leaves.

6

Among the letters and papers on my desk I noticed a little card. I reached for it and found it was an invitation to a party from some professional body. I got up quickly, went down to my car and drove to the place where the party was being held.

I went into a large hall and saw sparkling lights and guests dressed in starched ironed clothes, with formal, strained expressions on their faces. I let my eyes rove around the place and the people as if I was looking for something in particular. The men were stealing glances at the women and the women at the men. I strolled among the guests nodding to them when they nodded to me, like a doll with its head on a spring.

There was a sudden commotion and the guests rushed forward, pushing each other aside, to crowd around a small corpulent man. They all wanted to walk next to him, be photographed with him, appear on television standing near him, and make him remember their faces, their voices, their existence.

I left the crush and stood in a quiet corner. I half

turned and found a man standing there. An ordinary man wearing ordinary clothes and standing in an ordinary way. He was neither short nor tall, thin nor fat, but I felt that something out of the ordinary hung about him. Perhaps it was that his expression was natural and relaxed, unlike the tense, starched features of those around him... perhaps that he was elegant in spite of his simplicity... perhaps that he scorned to join the group clustering round the man...

He looked in my direction and his eyes met mine. I felt a vague stirring inside. His eyes smiled faintly. He said in a voice which was almost as lively as his eyes, 'They're running after him.'

'Why?' I asked simply.

'He's the head of the corporation.'

He stood watching the people for a few moments with the same faint smile in his eyes. Was it a look of scorn or compassion, respect for human frailty or derision? I couldn't decide. He turned back and looked hard at me for a moment before introducing himself. I reciprocated, telling him who I was and what I did. Pointing to a small table placed a little apart from the others, he said, 'Let's sit here. It's the furthest table from the head man.'

We both laughed and went over to the table and sat facing each other. He looked at the plates of food, then at me and said smiling, 'I'm not very good at knowing what to do at parties. Can I help you to something?'

What was it in this man's eyes?

'No thank you,' I said. 'I don't like party manners.'

We started eating in silence and after a while he asked, 'Do you find time to listen to music?'

'Not often,' I replied. 'I haven't heard your latest composition but I read how successful it was and how much people liked it.'

His eyes strayed far away from me, then he looked at me again and said, 'I wasn't happy with it.'

'But the public was.'

'An artist isn't content unless he himself is satisfied with what he's done.'

'Why did you allow something to be broadcast if you weren't completely happy with it?'

'That's what's so agonizing. The work that I'm pleased with, the public doesn't understand.'

'So why don't you compose pieces that you're happy with, regardless of how the public reacts?'

'Who'd listen to them?'

'A few people. Just one... But that's better than satisfying the public at any cost.'

'I do that sometimes.'

He looked down at the floor briefly, as if thinking, then raised his expressive eyes to me and said, 'We've talked about music a lot. Why haven't you mentioned medicine?'

'Conversations about medicine aren't appropriate for parties,' I said.

'Why not?' he asked in surprise.

'It's all about pain and sickness. The sad side of life,' I replied.

'No,' he argued. 'Of course the sorrows involved are immense, but the happiness must be even greater.

I can imagine how happy you must feel when you save someone's life. That must be the best part of your work.'

'What about yours? What's the part of your work that gives you the most happiness?'

'When I write a tune that pleases me,' he answered. 'Or when I hear some magnificent piece of music.'

Then he looked at me and added, smiling, 'Or when I make a new friend.'

I tried to avoid his eyes but he wouldn't let me escape and encompassed me confidently within his gaze. My heart gave a single frightening lurch.

★ ★ ★ ★

I turned over and over, unable to sleep. The bed seemed to be full of stones and nails. I got up and started walking about the room. It seemed cramped and cell-like and the air throttled me like a hangman's rope. I went out on to the balcony and stood for a while but then I couldn't bear it any more so I sat down. That too became intolerable and I went into the dining-room. I tried to eat something but the food tasted rubbery and odd.

Everything had become unbearable: sitting, standing, walking, eating. Food, water and air had lost their savour for me. The things that used to take up my time seemed trivial and meaningless. My new feeling replaced my former preoccupations and consumed my waking hours with its intensity. One series of questions wandered constantly through the regions of my mind and soul: should I try to contact him, talk to him, be the one to initiate the conversation?

I looked at the little instrument: the squarish black lump of plastic I used to carry about from place to place, and to silence with one finger if I felt like it, had become an object of terror, a dangerous bewitching piece of equipment. I looked warily at it from a distance, approached it apprehensively, and when I touched it a powerful electric charge went through me as if I'd touched a naked wire. Do things change to such an extent when our view of them changes?

I sat beside the telephone thinking. I remembered what he'd said when he wrote his number down for me: 'Call me when you want to.'

He'd shown respect for my ability to decide, so why couldn't I? I always had done in the past. Wasn't it my will rather than the will of another which had controlled me? Hadn't a man tried to possess my life and been unable to because I hadn't wanted him to? And another had tried to give me his life and I hadn't taken a thing from him because I hadn't wanted to. My will had always determined my giving and taking. I wanted to see him now. Yes, I wanted to.

I turned my index finger in the holes on the disc six times and the repeated high-pitched tone sounded in my ears. Suddenly it was broken off and the flow of blood to my heart stopped momentarily. I heard his deep voice saying, 'Hello.'

I didn't think about different ways to be flirtatious or take refuge in womanly evasiveness. I didn't pretend that I was just phoning to ask something. I didn't veil my face and signal to him from behind my door, or act naive and stupid. I said truthfully, 'I want to see you.'

'When?'

'Now.'

'Where?'

'Anywhere. The place isn't important.'

'Where are you now?'

'At home.'

'I'll be with you as soon as I can.'

I sat back in the chair as if the life had drained out of me and looked about me at the furniture and the walls as if I were seeing them for the first time.

Suddenly I was seized with energy and enthusiasm: this picture ought to be over here; the chair ought to be there; the vase should be full of flowers. I sent the servant to buy a bunch of flowers, then put on an apron and went into the kitchen to make a cake with fresh eggs and milk. While it was in the oven I made a jelly and put it in the fridge. I raced about like a child from the oven to the fridge, the fridge to the vase, the vase to the picture on the wall, and back to the oven.

Sweat poured down my face and ran into my mouth but it somehow had a delicious new taste. My chest rose and fell in staccato, panting breaths like a racehorse, but I'd forgotten about my lungs. I put my hand in the oven and didn't feel the heat, as if my brain cells had forgotten the pain of burning. My back was twisted from bending down under tables and hunching over work-surfaces as if my backbone didn't exist. Then the doorbell gave one long ring which echoed strangely and alarmingly in my heart as if I were hearing it for the first time in my life.

★ ★ ★ ★

He sat in the sitting-room; his deep eyes, still smiling, strayed over the pictures on the walls and his composed, serious features registered curiosity and interest as he looked about him. I sat a little way from him trying to conceal the strange feeling stirring in my insides, suppressing the unfamiliar joy in my heart and trying to ignore the violent trembling of my soul. But how could I, when my eyes, lips and voice all betrayed me? He smiled gently and said, 'Your house is beautiful — the house of an artist.'

'I love art,' I said, 'but medicine takes up all my time.'

'Medicine's an art in itself,' he said, and looked at me.

What was it in this man's eyes? A deep, bottomless sea?

'Would you like some tea?' I asked him and he nodded slightly, smiling. I left him and went to make the tea. The servant stared at me in doubtful surprise — I was doing something in the kitchen for the first time since I'd come to live there. I took the cake out of the oven and put it on the plate next to the tea and went back in to him. He looked at the newly baked cake — which was obviously still underdone — and smiled. But I couldn't help laughing and he began to laugh with me, and we laughed as if we'd never stop. This natural unrestrained laughter tore the fine veil of inhibition still separating us, and he looked me straight in the eye and said, 'I've never met a woman like you before.'

'What do you mean?'

'Women always hide their feelings and wear masks on their faces so you don't know what they're really like. But you don't hide anything. You don't even wear make-up.'

'I like myself as I am, and I rely on myself being as I am so I can't pretend I'm different.'

'I like a woman who's honest and open.'

'A lot of men think that openness in a woman spoils her femininity. They like her to wear disguises, to be evasive, to join with them in the game of chasing and being chased.'

'Then they see women solely as a source of sexual pleasure.'

'There aren't many men who understand the femininity of an intelligent woman with a strong personality.'

'I think', he said, 'that however beautiful a woman's body is, she isn't truly feminine if she's stupid or weak or affected or insincere.'

'What about masculinity?' I asked.

'Most women think that masculinity just means whether a man's good at sex.'

'In my opinion,' I said, 'however good he may be at sex, a man isn't masculine if he's stupid or weak or affected or insincere.'

'Where've you been all these years?' he asked.

'Busy searching.'

'What for?'

'Lots of things.'

'Didn't you find what you were looking for?'

'Never.'

'We can't have everything in life.'

'I've lived in a state of permanent deprivation.'

'Deprivation tightens the nerve strings so you can play on them. If you're satisfied they grow slack and you can't produce a tune.'

He was talking to me, looking into my eyes all the time. I never once saw him stare at my thighs or glance stealthily at my breasts. We were alone. The four walls closed around us. But I didn't feel that he was seeing the walls or feeling them. He was on another plane and I was beside him in flesh and blood. Yet I never felt he was addressing my body. He was directing himself to my heart and mind.

I closed my eyes, feeling calm and secure.

★ ★ ★ ★

I sat beside him and watched his long clever fingers holding the plectrum and moving over the zither with confident expertise. He played notes that soared in the air and notes that sank down low... sad notes and happy notes... notes that shouted and whispered, laughed and cried... And my heart was with them beat for beat, rising and sinking, dancing and weeping, groaning and laughing.

His fingers stopped and he asked, 'What do you think?'

'It's wonderful.'

'I've just written it.'

'It's got tears in it, and it's got joy.'

'That's life!'

'How beautiful art is. If only I'd studied music so I could write tunes like that!'

'If only I'd studied medicine so that I could heal people!'

'Medicine only heals. Art heals and creates.'

'You could be creative in medicine. There are illnesses which no one's found a cure for yet.'

I looked at him: 'Where have you been all these years?'

'Looking for you.'

'Have you tried with others?'

'Of course. And you?'

'Of course.'

'It's the only way to find out.'

I heard his deep voice calling to me. 'What is it about your eyes?' he asked. We stood opposite each other with only a single pace separating us and I heard him saying in his warm voice, 'I love you.'

Everything in me rushed downwards to some deep distant spot, then soared to the highest peak of my being. He smiled and covered the distance between us and slowly took me in his arms. I rested my head on his chest.

'Why are you crying?' he asked.

'I love you.'

He held me close and embraced me until all my being melted into his and his whole existence was lost in mine.

The loud ringing of the telephone brought me down from heaven to earth. I jumped up and went over to it: 'Hello.'

An anxious voice came over the line: 'Save him, doctor. He's dying.'

Still holding the receiver, I looked at him and he asked immediately, 'A patient?'

'Yes.'

'Are you going?'

'Straightaway.'

'Shall I come with you?'

'If you like.'

I got into his car beside him and he drove off at speed. We reached the patient's house, which wasn't a house at all but a small damp room in a dark basement at the bottom of a block of flats. A thin young man lay on a dirty mattress on the floor. Beside him was a little pool of blood. I sounded his chest, realizing he was desperately ill with pulmonary tuberculosis and that his life depended on a blood transfusion. I looked round and found my companion standing beside me. He said instantly, 'Do you need anything?'

'A bottle of blood straightaway from the emergency services.'

He ran towards the door saying, 'I'll take the car and bring the blood straight back.'

I sat on a wooden crate beside the patient and

injected him to give him some temporary relief, then prepared the blood transfusion equipment. He came rushing back in with the bottle of blood in his hand. I jumped up; he held the patient's arm and stayed beside me helping until I'd got the needle firmly fixed in the vein.

I looked at him. Sweat was pouring down his face and he was squatting with his head close to the sick man's head. I whispered in his ear, 'Move away from him.'

'Why?'

'You might catch it.'

'What about you?'

'It's my job. I have to do it regardless of the conditions.'

He looked at me in silence and didn't move until I'd finished setting up the transfusion equipment.

We sat side by side on the wooden crate watching the drops of blood flowing from the bottle to the tube to the man's vein with anxious haste as if they were alive and shared our desperation to save his life.

I looked at him and he smiled gently without speaking. I said, 'I couldn't have done all that alone.'

'Yes, you could.' Then he pointed at the bottle and said, 'There's only a little bit left.'

I looked at the sick man's eyes and they were focusing better. His breathing was slower and more regular. I took the needle out and he parted his lips and said 'Thanks' in a dry voice, looking at both of us. Then he stuck his hand weakly under his dirty pillow and stretched out his thin arm to me clutching a pound note in his fist.

I don't know what happened to me at that point. The world spun round and I felt ready to faint. I was aware only of a hand supporting me and him saying tenderly, 'Are you tired?'

I looked at him and didn't know what to say: I wasn't tired, I just felt deeply embarrassed and ashamed. Perhaps it was the oddness and squalor of the situation that had upset me, but I felt at that moment that it was not honourable, just or logical for a doctor to take a fee from a patient. How had I held out my hand all these years and taken money from my patients? How had I sold health to people in my surgery? How could I have filled my coffers from the blood and sweat of the sick?

I felt his hand supporting me out of the building and guiding me to the car. Then he drove me home. When he'd seen me to bed he asked smiling, 'Shall I call a doctor?' and I felt the tears stinging my face. 'What's wrong?' he said, taking my hand.

'I didn't understand anything. I was blind. All I could see was myself. The battles I was fighting hid the truth from me.'

'What battles?'

'Battles against everybody, starting with my mother.'

'Didn't you achieve anything?'

'No...'

No, I hadn't achieved a thing. Being a doctor wasn't a case of diagnosing the illness, prescribing the medicine and grabbing the money. Success didn't mean filling the surgery, getting rich and having my name in lights. Medicine wasn't a commodity and success was not to be measured in terms of money and fame.

Being a doctor meant giving health to all who needed it, without restrictions or conditions, and success was to give what I had to others.

Thirty years of my life had gone by without my realizing the truth, without my understanding what life was about or realizing my own potential. How could I have done, when I'd only thought about taking? — although I couldn't have given something which I didn't have to give.

'Try to sleep,' he said looking at me lovingly.

'I can't.'

'He'll get better once the blood's had its effect.'

'He'll never get better.'

'You didn't take the money.'

'Don't remind me... '

As if I could forget! The cramped basement room, the dirty mattress on the tiles, the pool of blood, the haggard face, the hollow eyes and that long skinny arm stretched out towards me clutching the knife that had cleaved my mind and heart in two.

I hid my face against his chest, seeking his protection, clinging to him. I felt as if I'd been stripped of my past life and had gone back to being a child learning to walk. I'd begun to need a hand to support me. For the first time in my life I felt that I needed someone else, something I hadn't felt even about my mother.

I buried my head in his chest and wept tears of quiet relief.